Henry and Mudge
TAKE THE
Big Test

The Tenth Book of Their Adventures

Story by Cynthia Rylant
Pictures by Suçie Stevenson

Ready-to-Read
Aladdin Paperbacks

To Jack and Sally Papp and all the good dogs they've trained   —CR
For Heidi Mitke and her own pup   —SS

THE HENRY AND MUDGE BOOKS

First Aladdin Paperbacks Edition, 1996

Text copyright © 1991 by Cynthia Rylant
Illustrations copyright © 1991 by Suçie Stevenson

Aladdin Paperbacks
An imprint of Simon & Schuster Children's Publishing Division
1230 Avenue of the Americas
New York, NY 10020

READY-TO-READ is a registered trademark of Simon & Schuster, Inc.
Also available in a Simon & Schuster Books for Young Readers Edition.

The text of this book was set in 18-point Goudy Old Style.
The illustrations were rendered in pen-and-ink and watercolor, reproduced in full color.

Series designed by Mina Greenstein.

Printed and bound in the United States of America

17 18 19 20

The Library of Congress has catalogued the hardcover edition as follows:
Rylant, Cynthia.
Henry and Mudge take the big test: the tenth book of their adventures / story by Cynthia Rylant;
pictures by Suçie Stevenson.
p.   cm.
Summary: After eight weeks at Papp's Dog School, Henry's dog Mudge earns a certificate and lots of
liver treats.
[1. Dogs—Training—Fiction.] I. Stevenson, Suçie, ill.
II. Title.
PZ7.R982Hlj   1991
[E]—dc20   90-35171
CIP   AC
ISBN-10: 0-689-81010-5 (hc.)
ISBN-13: 978-0-689-80886-9 (Aladdin pbk.)
ISBN-10: 0-689-80886-0 (Aladdin pbk.)

Contents

The Smart Dog

On a sunny day
Henry and Henry's mother
and Henry's big dog Mudge
were sitting on their front porch.
A man with a collie walked by.

Suddenly the man stopped.

"Sit," said the man.

The collie sat.

"Down," said the man.

The collie lay down.

Henry looked at Mudge.

Mudge looked at Henry.

They both looked at the collie.

"Stay," said the man.
Then he walked a long way
down the street.
He didn't look back.
The collie stayed.

The man turned down another street
and disappeared.
The collie stayed.

After a while the man came back.
"Susie, heel," he said to the collie,
and they walked down the street together.

Henry looked at his mother.

"Wow," he said.

"Smart dog," she said.

Henry looked at Mudge.

"Mudge, heel," said Henry, and he walked down the steps.

Mudge rolled over
and started to drool.

"Well, at least he's good
at staying," Henry said.

"Except when company comes,"
said Henry's mother.
"Right." Henry frowned.
"And when the cat next door
wants to visit," said Henry's mother.
"Right." Henry frowned some more.

"And when your dad is mowing the grass," said Henry's mother.

"Right." Henry frowned even more.

"Maybe Mudge needs to go to school,"
Henry said to his mother.

"Maybe."

"Maybe Mudge needs a nice teacher
like Mrs. Crocus," Henry said.

Mrs. Crocus was Henry's second
grade teacher.

"Maybe." Henry's mother smiled.

"Mudge," said Henry, "do you
want to go to school?"
Mudge snored and drooled.
"I hope dog school has nap time,"
said Henry.
"And lots of paper towels,"
said Henry's mother, looking
at her porch.

School

DOG LEASHES

COLLARS

B

LARGE

ME

Henry went shopping for
Mudge's first day of school.

He bought Mudge a new red leash.

He bought Mudge a new silver collar.

He bought Mudge a box of liver treats.

And Henry bought himself
a paddle-ball because
he was nervous.
Henry liked to play paddle-ball
when he was nervous.
And he was nervous
because he thought Mudge
might flunk dog school.

He thought Mudge might
drool on the teacher's foot.
Or sit on a poodle by mistake.

Or not even stay awake long enough
to do anything.
Henry paddled like crazy.

When the first day of school
arrived, Henry and Henry's mother
and Henry's big dog Mudge
drove to a long white building.
Its sign read: "Papp's Dog School."

Inside was Jack Papp with a
handful of dog treats.
"Mr. Papp is your teacher,"
Henry told Mudge.
Mudge wagged.
He jumped up to lick Jack Papp's face.
"No Mudge!" said Henry.

"Don't worry," said Jack Papp.

"I know what to do."

He held Mudge's front paws.

He wouldn't let go.

He danced Mudge up.

He danced Mudge back.

He danced Mudge all around.

Mudge didn't like dancing.
When Jack Papp finally let go,
Mudge didn't jump up again.
He was afraid Jack might
want to dance.

"Pretty good teacher,"
Henry said to his mother.
"Pretty good," she said.
They watched Jack Papp give Mudge
a dog treat and a hug.
So far dog school was fun.

The Big Test

Mudge was not a perfect student.

He liked to lie down too much.

He liked to sniff the other students.

He liked to think about other things.

But he always showed up.

And he always wagged his tail.

And he always gave his teacher a kiss.

At home Henry practiced with Mudge.

They practiced in the backyard.

Henry had one pocket full of liver treats.

When Mudge did something right,

he got a treat.

When Mudge did something wrong,

he got "Aw, Mudge."

And after a few weeks
Henry needed *two* pockets
full of liver treats
because Mudge was getting almost
everything right.
He sat when he heard "Sit."
He walked when he heard "Heel."
And he stayed when he heard "Stay."
Most of the time, anyway.
He still didn't do too well
when the cat next door came to visit.

Henry and Mudge went to dog class
for eight weeks.
They worked very hard.
They went through many boxes of liver treats.

The last day of class was the big test.

Henry and Henry's parents and

Henry's big dog Mudge arrived early.

Jack Papp would decide which dogs

passed the test.

He said that Mudge would go after

the beagle and before the chow chow.

"Good dog, Mudge," whispered Henry.

"We can do it."

When it was their turn,

Jack Papp said to Mudge,

"Okay, Mudge, let's see what you can do."

Jack Papp gave Henry a big smile.

"Sit," said Henry.

Mudge sat.

"Down," said Henry.

Mudge lay down.

"Stay," said Henry.

Mudge stayed.

Henry walked away.

He didn't look back.

He walked around the long white building,

wishing he had his

paddle-ball.

He sure hoped Mudge would stay. . .

Mudge did stay!

When Henry came back

he saw Mudge lying in the same place,

wagging his tail.

He gave Mudge a big hug

and a kiss and two liver treats.

Henry shook Jack Papp's hand.

Mudge shook Jack Papp's hand.

Mudge had passed the test.

He got a fancy certificate.

He got a gold ribbon.

He got a giant dog biscuit.

Henry's father and Henry's mother
clapped and clapped.

"Wow," said Henry's father.

"Smart dog," said Henry's mother.

"Great dog," said Henry.

Mudge wagged at them
and barked
and drooled one last time
on his teacher's foot.